the End of the Closet

Curiosity

Vincent R. Petrucci

Inks and Bindings
888-290-5218
www.inksandbindings.com
orders@inksandbindings.com

Contents

The End of The Closet

I was always at my Nonna's house as a child growing up. They were really not the best housekeepers, yet they had everything in the house that Nonno built. My grandparents were hardworking immigrants from Italy. Most of their time and energy were spent in the fields farming grapes and other crops. They were farmers and great people. I enjoyed being there collecting eggs or working in their gardens that were full of beautiful tomatoes and other vegetables. The house was simple yet it had many rooms, one bathroom, laundry room, three bedrooms, kitchen, basement and attic. It also had a dirty kitchen where Nonno would make his cheese and butter or hang huge prosciutto. It was all there.

One bedroom in that farmhouse was really peculiar. There was a joining closet where my Nonno slept. There was a closet door and if you walked in the big closet and turned right you would enter the next room. The walk-in closet was nice, yet nothing fancy. My Nonna slept in the adjoining room. It was a beautiful, simple room. You could always smell the powder my Nonna would wear. She was not the type to use makeup, yet was a beautiful woman. She naturally spent her time in the corn fields and vineyards— picking fruits, peaches, apricots plums etc. It also had a gorgeous shining bedspread. I can still see that turquoise image … It was like a secret door through one room to the other. As a young kid, I liked to play there.

There were so many items in the closet beside clothes— money, coffee, cans full of money, folders, empty coffee cans, dollars, quarters, lots of money for an 8-yr old kid. You can also see books, guns, bullets, shotgun shells, some old coats, maybe one suit or so, not really any dresses and stacks of papers.

One day, I was playing back there but my Nonno really didn't want anyone in the back rooms. It was cold in the winter and hot in the summer in those back bedrooms. The front room is where everyone ate and watched tv and or carried on conversation. In that room, there was a cooling system for the hot summer or the wood stove for the winter. Most of my time was spent here in the front room. There was also a living room, yet I rarely went there. He had locks on the doors yet I knew where the keys were even back then. One day, while I was there playing, instead of turning right and going out the door to my Nonna's room, I turned left. It was my first time exploring that end of the closet. There were so many obstacles in the way. It was not easy to get back to my Nonno's room. It was off limits so I really had not been in there many times.

One morning, I was going to start to explore the north end of the closet. After moving small items, at first glance, I remember seeing what appeared to be a door. There was a lock on it. The door was small — not the average size door. You see, my Nonno was a very intelligent and a handy person. Besides being a farmer, he was a carpenter. One friend of the family stated to me, "Your Nonno could have been anything he wanted, even a doctor. He was bright, hardworking and driven". One hot summer day, while I was playing in the closet, I heard my Nonno walking down the hall with his bastone. I was small and clever and was able to get out of the closet and his room before he found me. I ended up around the corner in the bathroom through the laundry room and back in the kitchen. Nonno greeted me. "What are you doing bimbo?", he asked. I replied, "I'm assisting my cousins washing dishes, Nonno". "Okay, Vincent, just don't go back to the bedrooms," he said laughingly. He knew I was a curious kid. He knew I liked to play there and take a few quarters.

It was not easy to get back to the bedroom. The house there was always occupied—Nonno or Nonna, some of the Mexican employees and my cousins, so going back in the closet was almost impossible. The house would be locked. The doors going to the back room were locked. Now I see the end of the closet door had a lock.

I wanted to go back to the left side of the closet. I had to find out what was on the other side of the small door. Was it another room? Was it another closet?

Days and weeks went by. I was always there around the ranch playing with my dogs and or catching frogs as an 8-yr old having fun.

Nonno who seemed older to me, yet still drives and smokes. He drank wine every single day, but never did I see him drunk. That day, the ambulance arrived. They took Nonno away that evening. The family visited Nonno at the hospital. Father stated his heart was not right, but assured me that he will be fine.

I was sad. I loved my Nonno. I was there almost every day. I ate, slept and played there. I also enjoyed my cousins' company. They would always come and wash the dishes. We played together and were just average kids, I guess.

The next day, I was at the ditch catching frogs. I stopped and thought, then decided to walk to my Nonno's house. It was just through the vineyards around a 1 mile walk. My parent's home was part of the farm's property. It all ran together and this was my backyard. Acres of vineyard to hunt, to catch frogs and to play with my dogs. I enjoyed shooting my daisy BB gun that my father bought though I was only 8 yrs. old. My father loved to hunt doves, ducks and pheasants. I went through my father's hunter's safety course and later would take the official class near our local airport.

I knew my Nonno was not home and my cousins were finished washing the dishes maybe by 2 pm. I thought of the idea a bit more and tried to enter the front door—it was open!

My uncle, a kind man who was not married and still lived with his parents, was working in the fields with our workers or perhaps at the hospital with my Nonno. I knew it was taboo, however, I wanted to continue to look over what I had found sometime 3 weeks ago.

I grabbed the key to the hall door. It was under the couch in my Nonno's old slippers. Wow! They were old. Then once in the hallway, I heard a truck and tractor coming in the yard. My heart was pounding. I was like in the middle of the house. I heard the front door open. It was Francisco. He was bringing in the mail. I was relieved. No more anxiety. The house door slammed shut as it always did. I felt the glass door would break but it never did.

I continued down the hallways into my Nonno's room. The door was open. I guess, with all of the confusion 2 days ago, with the ambulance coming to the farm, all of the doors that were normally locked were now all open.

I quickly moved through the can's full money and the obstacles in the way. It was hard even for a 8-yr old to maneuver in this closet. Tons of things in the way. I approached the end and saw the door. This small door was hidden. Who knew about the door, my father, my Nonno, my uncle, Nonna, my cousins? My father, he had been brought up in this house, he must have known.

Once there, I discovered the door knob was not new. It was like an old antique. I tried opening the door but it was locked. I knew it would be. Where would I find the key? This was an old type of key hole. So many keys hidden in so many slippers and old coffee cans for many sheds and barns and truck tractors. I would never find this key. The hole was shaped like a body with a big hole at the top then thin, all the way down.

The front door opened. It was uncle. I could hear him tell one of our workers he would use the bathroom and be out. I stayed there for 1/2 an hour, later after using the bathroom then eating some of my Nonno's stacks of 2 or 3-days old pancakes with homemade jelly, my uncle would go back outside. Uncle ate a lot. He was not super fat yet was a little fat.

He was a nice uncle, however gets upset easily when someone doesn't follow instructions …It seems like he was missing something in his life.

I left the house and went back home. It was then summertime. The sun was hot. I went to the ditch yet became bored and hot. I went for a swim at my parent's home. I was fixated on the door and finding the key.

Happy Days

Time passed, the summer was always full of adventure going to 4-H camp with my sister and friends swimming with the browns that lived down the road. I stayed busy. Played a lot of wiffle ball and baseball. At times, I would visit my other cousins in town.

It was just what kids did that lived in the country on a family farm. Most of the time, I would go down to my Nonno's to have lunch. My Nonno and my cousins and or their Nonna's would make some lunch.

I knew Nonno was still in the hospital, it had been 2 days now. My uncle was talking to his aunt, Zia Tina, he stated that my Nonno would be back tomorrow. Wow, that lady never did like me. I never will forget the days my cousins were here from Italy. You see, Zia would call on the phone even though her house was only 40 yards away from my Nonno's just to say that coffee and cookies were ready. So, my uncle would go there each day after lunch, but I was never invited to have coffee and cookies even when my cousin was here from Italy. I did not at the time speak Italian yet was looked at as less because my mother was not Italian. In fact, her dog also hated me. BB was the dog's name. I could not enter that house from the back door. The dog would tear me up. Zia would always say, "Vincent was *cattivo* i.e., naughty". She appeared old to me as well, I respected her, my father always insisted to respect her family.

Well, it appeared that my Nonno would be back the next day. I was content. I loved my Nonno room. Even though he did not speak English, I communicated well with him. I spoke a few Italian words.

My cousins came over that day and washed dishes and were going to tidy up my Nonno's room, prior to him returning home. Not a lot yet, clean sheets. It might have been the first clean sheet in weeks. They were just not into the whole house cleaning. They worked in the fields and kept their crops growing. That was the priority of my Nonno.

So, I saw the slippers being pulled from under the couch by my cousin to unlock the door going down to the hallways to my Nonno's room. I was playing with the dog and noticed at a glance a long body key. It was an old key. It was not like the others. I really thought it was the key to the little door at the north end of the closet. A good feeling came over me.

Nonno is Back

What a beautiful day it was. Nonno was back home. You could see contentment on the family's faces. Nonno's home and feeling better. Nonno was the patriarch of the family.

He was stern. He ruled, yet was a fair man. I do not believe I ever remember my Nonno left the farm unless he was going to another ranch or to the doctor. So, all the family had a great deal of respect for him. Some friends would come and visit him. They would sit outside, smoke and drink a half a glass of his homemade red wine.

It appeared nothing had happened to Nonno at the hospital. He was there smoking again. He started to cook his pizza and all was normal. I loved that pizza. The nice baker from town would bring my Nonno pizza dough and my Nonno would give him fresh homemade red wine. Salvadore was his name. So, I continued to come each day to have lunch. My father was so happy when I was there.

Nonno on the first few days after hospitalization would walk slowly down the hall with his bastone and sleep a bit after lunch. He would ask my cousin to get his keys. When I saw my cousin reach down for the old slipper again, I saw the odd-looking key. That was it. That was the key. I then knew that the key was there. I would wait a few days. Each day I came for lunch,

I checked the slipper. The key was there. Today, I would take the key. Tomorrow after lunch and during the time my cousins were washing dishes, I would go to the closet. Nonno would always go out on the porch and smoke post lunch and before coffee with his sister.

That was my chance. I had the key and I went down the hall. My heart was always racing while walking in the back rooms. It even smelled different in those rooms. There were not a lot of things there. I walked into the closet from my Nonno's room then I turned left. I moved all the things in my way. I was there. I had the key. This 8-yr old kid, there I was.

I put the key in the odd-shaped lock. It would not turn. I shook it a bit as uncle always did when things did not work and of course used a few choice words and lifted up on the door knob. It clicked. Oh, wow! I opened the secret door to who knows and what was there.

It was dark inside like no windows even though it was the middle of summer and 2 pm, but so dark like underground. I saw a pull string light. I pulled the string. The light was on.

There it was. All these small couches and what seemed to be a small ottoman is in a hallway leading to the unknown. The area was painted in bright red and green and looked a bit like my Nonna's bedspread, almost turquoise. It had the same smell of my Nonna's room— that powder she used after taking a shower.

I heard my cousins telling my Nonno they were finished with washing the dishes. I needed to leave. Wow! I had finally made it to the entry of the room. The floor seemed to slope in a downward direction. It was almost like a tunnel. It really was warm and dry, but was not dirty and felt as if someone had been there recently.

I made it back down the hallway through the kitchen and back outside. No one knew I was there. The only issue was I still had the key and needed to place it back in the old slipper.

That would not be hard since I had a plan.

The summer days were long. It stayed light outside until nearly 9pm. Lots of swimming and playing near the ditch. Catching frogs, exploring and riding my old buckskin colored horse, Jake. What a nice horse yet did buck me off a few times. The next morning, I went with my Nonna and some of the Mexican workers to pick fruits in the fields. Apricots were ready since it was late June.

The farm had several trees that were mature. Nonna and the workers had long sticks and would hit the branches then the fruit would fall to the ground.

We had small buckets and would gather the fruit then transfer them into the 50lb lug wooden boxes. From there, we would drive the tractor and trailer back to my Nonna's.

My cousins would be there with their Nonna. We would now cut the apricots and prepare to dry them in the huge smoke and or sulfur house that Nonno built. This is just like every other structure on the farm. The only time is when Nonno would have Angelo come and paint. Angelo was an old man. It seemed to me everyone was old except for my father and mother. Nonno did it all. This was a pretreatment for the fruit and would prevent them from spoilage and or becoming dark.

My childhood was like this — working on the farm. I was out there in short pants, no shirt and thongs on my feet and my skin was dark brown all summer.

The next morning, I was going to place the key back in the old slipper. I was only hoping my Nonno was not looking for the key. That day at lunch, though I didn't understand Italian much, I heard my Nonno mentioned to my uncle something about a key. "Chiave," I heard that word and knew the meaning. I saw him shake his head. No! Then my Nonno laughed a bit and said something like dio cane mexicanna.

I felt then my Nonno had gone to look for the key, yet maybe did not find it so I decided to place the key back, but this time not inside the shoe. I would put the key to the side. This way Nonno would think the key could have fallen outside the slipper or perhaps he missed putting it inside.

After lunch that day, my cousins came over to wash the dishes. I would assist them and play with them. We were friends; however, I knew their Nonna had always said not to get close to Vincent, he was cattivo.

Nonno was smoking half of his old cigarette. He never would smoke the entire cigarette, then later would light it up. The same with his glass of wine. He drinks half glass or less then leaves the glass there with wine in it then later would pick it up. I guess that is why it was so hard to clean those small glasses from the wine stain. All his homemade vino bouno actually was good wine. I enjoyed a sip myself each day.

Nonno called one of my cousins from the kitchen and I heard him ask, "Can you see if there is a key under the couch in the slipper?" Nonno really did not trust me. Again, I felt because I was not full-blooded Italian and my cousin at the time spoke a few words in Italian and both parents were Italian. Well, he trusted them more than me.

I saw my cousin say, "Oh! Vincenzo, the key was outside the slipper. Maybe when you put it back, it fell out." My Nonno was happy and laughed and was hitting his bastone on the floor.

My plan had worked. No one was suspicious. I had found the key went in the room. Now, the key is back. I would wait a few days and then continue to explore the room.

We had a great 4th of July that year. Our friends down the road would have a barbeque. We always walked down the road south. It was just less than a mile. I always liked the parties there, especially the girls—they were so cute and were also half Italians. Their mother was Italian and father was from Illinois, I believe.

Their mother was a small woman—very dark. She enjoyed cleaning the yard outside in her bathing suit. At times, I would walk down the road and assist her pushing the wheelbarrow full of grass into the vineyard rows.

The next morning was bright and sunny. I went with my father to change the water in some sweet corn. Oh! I hated to pick that corn.

Dad would always say wear long sleeve shirts and boots, yet it was so hot and the corn would shed fine hair on you and would itch a lot. Oh well, I would jump in the swimming pool and all was well.

Lunch at Nonno's pizza and liver. I loved the liver Nonno prepared. He had just killed a young cow along with his homemade pizza.

Today is going to be the day. I am going to get the key and go back into the room. I knew post lunch, Nonno would take a nap at the table and or walk out on the porch. He would just put his head down and sleep right there. Nonna was there yet quietly reading. Uncle would go to Zia's house for coffee. Post coffee would lay on the old couch and sleep, yet not before consuming 2 or 3 biscotti that my cousins had made. That was my chance. I did not have a lot of time. The first step was getting the key. I knew Nonno had a doctor's appointment that afternoon. My uncle would take him. My cousins had come and started washing the dishes at my Nonno's.

I would thank my Nonno and walk home through the vineyard and across the small bridge, swim and cool off. I had unlocked the back door at my Nonno's house. It was from the backyard where my Nonno's pizza oven was located.

Second Time Around

Two pm in the afternoon, the sun was hot. I rode my bike down the long road to my Nonno's. As I entered the driveway, I could see my uncle leaving at the other end of the ranch which was half a mile away. All the dust from his car that he never used was trailing him. I left my bike in the area near the 5 acres.

I jumped over the fence and walked to the back door.

I saw the back door was still open. The screen door with no lock and the glass and wood door. I walked straight in. The house was quiet and still smelled the pizza we had for lunch.

I moved the couch and stuck my hand underneath. I pulled out the slipper. There it was, the golden key. I tired the hallway door. Oh wow! It was locked so I went out the kitchen and into the dirty kitchen area through the laundry room and bathroom. I was in the middle room and walked over to my Nonna's room. She was out. Nobody was there.

I moved all the items away. Clothes can of money etcetera. There it was the small door entering into the room. I had been there one time yet not enough time. Today, I would return.

I put the key into the door. Yes! it opened click. Whoever built this door had done a precise job even though all the materials did not match. The key fits and the hinges were level, door opens with a little shake. I instantly smelled the powder that my Nonna always wore.

I reached for the small cord to turn on the light. Oh wow, the light bulb was out. My god! I froze for a second and then knew where the extra bulbs were located. They were not new bulbs yet still had some life in them.

You see nothing in the house and or on the farm was new. My family bought everything used. They did not believe in buying anything new. They would go to army surplus sales and buy tractors tools and anything else they could find.

All the meat was from the farm, chicken, beef, and pork. The family was what you called self-contained. They rarely bought any clothes. The shoes sometimes they would buy a new pair of rubber boots to change the water in the vineyards. In fact, every time they bought something new, it was a big deal. My uncle and or Nonno would make a remark on how nice it was. The family showed a lot of humility.

I put in the new bulb. Yes, it worked! I walked into the secret room. I saw all the turquoise-colored couches, I say a lot because there were 3 couches. Then there were nice ottomans with them. Some still had the plastic on them like they had never ever been used. I started noticing all these newspaper clippings and articles on the wall. They were framed. Somebody had a great interest in these articles. In my Nonno's entire house, there was nothing on the wall except nails with keys hanging on them. Very few pictures and or decorative items. I was only 8 yet could read. The print was bold. It talked about the catholic church. Wow! There was the priest that was at all of our Italian parties, Father M and then there was another priest in the pictures. I did not recognize this man. I saw Father M and he was a nice man always played tricks at the Italian parties. He

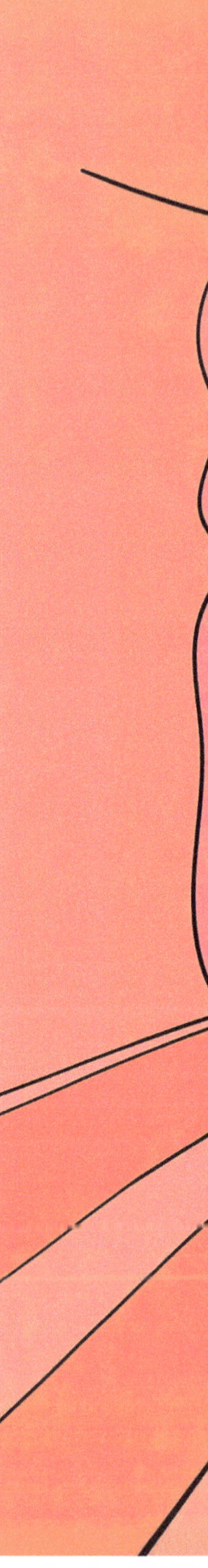

loved to sing, drink wine and smoke cigarettes. He was cool. However, I did not know the other man. He was also in a priest uniform.

My father was Catholic. My mother would always take my sister and myself to the Methodist Church. Yes, I would attend the catholic church on some occasions yet most of the time with my mother.

My father did not attend church much. Maybe on easter and or on Christmas. Sometimes we would go later in the night on Christmas and with my Italian cousins. It seemed they always looked down on me when we attended the catholic church. We were not following the kneeling act. They were not accepting me in the Italian community. After all, we were only half Italian. I felt this growing up. I felt this even with my father's friends.

I tried to read to the articles. It looked as if the bold print stated, dark blood in the church.

Then it showed Father M and the other priest. What was the fine print stating? I was not able to read all this. I just knew it must be something important. It was on the wall in the secret room. A little further down the circulating hallways was another print from the newspaper. It showed a small baby. I could see, it was a baby girl. The one priest along with Father M was holding the baby. They were smiling. Wow! There was my Nonno and Nonna young in those pictures along with my father and my uncle.

What was this picture? I really could not read it.

I had dictionary at home. I was starting to use it. I was turning 9 y.o. so was able to read. I heard a car approaching. It seemed we were at ground level inside the room. There was a vent next to the framed pictures. The room felt like it was underground so the car was easily heard.

I heard a horn. It was too early for my Nonno to be home. It may be somebody to buy fruit and or hay.

It was time for me to leave. I made my way out of the house. I would be back to the room yet this time would need more time. I would bring my dictionary. I wanted to read these strange newspaper articles on the wall.

The entire house had no pictures, but why were these there? Who was going in this room?

It smelled like my Nonna. The few pieces of furniture were the same color of my Nonna's bedspread. What was the significance of these pictures?

End of Summer

4th of July had come and gone. August was approaching. The harvest would soon start. I would assist driving the tractor, while the Mexican workers picked grapes. I always enjoyed being out in the fields, so free and so hot. I loved the sun on my skin. My mother would always tell me, "You are as brown as a little ginger bread boy Vincent. I love you, Vincent Ray." I loved my mother.

Each day, I was out with my Nonna to pick grapes. I was thinking of the secret room. I planned to go back inside next week. I knew there would be a party at my Nonno's sister's home. That would be the perfect time. They would all be dancing and eating. Salvadore would bring over his guitar and my uncle would have his harmonica. The other Italians, Lito and Clementina would be there with their family.

Wow! Clementina loved to sing this song called "Maria". Even her son, Marcello and his sister would sing. At times, their uncle Rolando would be on the roof singing and just acting crazy. It was a great life.

The time was right. I would bring my small dictionary. I was starting to use it last school year.

Party

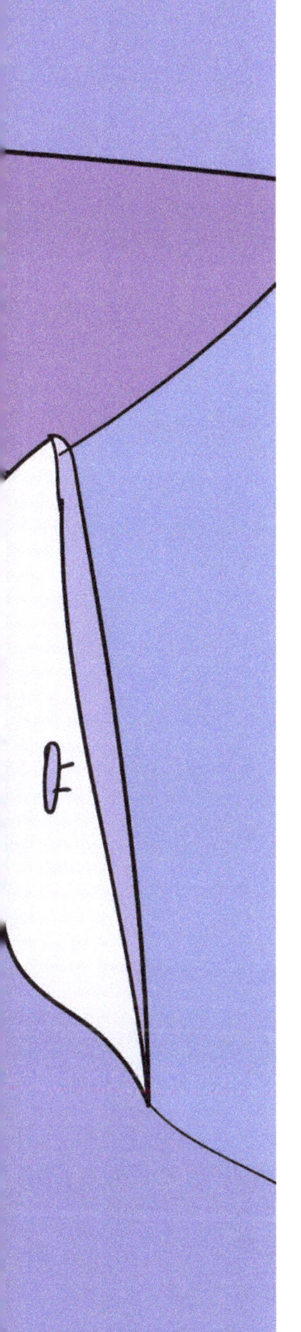

onna and Nonno would have parties at their home once in a blue moon.

They rarely had an event. The everyday life had plenty of people coming into the farm. Lots of Mexican employees would come and go. My Nonno's friends come in the afternoon to drink wine, talk about farming, etc.

However, the big parties with the Italians did not happen often. It took place that Saturday evening. Nonno and Francisco were barbequing lamb on my Nonno's make shift barbeque pit. It was really simple, but worked well made out of vineyard post and chicken wire.

My father's aunt and her daughter were preparing pasta and other delicious foods. Lito and Clementina that lived around 1 mile west came later. Clementina always made wonderful desserts. Sal brought his guitar and the party was on.

At 7 pm, the sun was still up. I had been playing with my cousins. I walked over to Nonno's house. I left my dictionary in the back garage area. All the guests and family were enjoying each other and deep into conversations.

I tried the back door in the dirty kitchen since it was always open. I went through the laundry room and into the old bathroom even at that time. Wow! The shower looked like a cave.

I went over to the couch and the odd-looking key was in the slipper. I walked down the hallway and went into Nonno's room and into the closet. I turned left and walked to the end. Each time I had been in the closet, I had moved books, coffee cans full of money, etc. It appeared nothing had changed since the last time I was here.

I put the key into the key hole, shook the door handle up and clicked it open. The pull string light worked. I saw all the couches and walked down the hallway around 20 feet. There were the picture frames on the wall on. There were bold letters. I took out my dictionary. Looked up the words mmm "scandal". Wow! Meaning, wrong or bad.

Catholic church local huge scandal! I continued to read as much as possible. Here, the next words showed abuse.

I continued to read, then was able to put the sentence together. The catholic church was under some investigation for abuse. It never really mentioned names, but there was Father M, who at that very moment was outside dancing and drinking. The other priest was also in the picture, but the picture didn't match the article. The 2 priests were in this picture, holding a baby.

The baby's name appears to say young Baby Petrucci, Gabriella. Who was this baby? In the background of the picture was my Nonno, my Nonna, my uncle, and my father, who at that time, were young boys.

Was this my aunt? Was this an unknown aunt that I never had heard about?

Wow! What were these newspaper articles doing here? Why was it a secret. As I walked a bit more down the hall, I noticed more articles. At the left side were candles lit and an area where there were several rosaries. I started to put things together. Father M was in middle of performing a baptism on this little newborn. The baby's name was Gabriella Petrucci. The other articles which showed that priests within the local church had been into abuse and that it was being investigated. Where was this baby? Wow! Now I read that the baby had died. Near the light of candles just up on the wall showed that here was a sudden death post baptism.

This secret room was a sanctuary. Who knows, yet I would say my Nonna was here praying on a regular basis. The candle had not burned much. The room was filled with the perfume and or powder my Nonna always used.

My father never really went to church. He always opposed giving money to Catholic church. This made sense. Did the priests have something to do with my aunt who I never knew and never heard about? I am just an 8-yr old kid. I am just a curious boy who has found what was behind the secret door.